Emmeline Pankhurst
Linda Hoy

Illustrated by
Julian Puckett

Hamish Hamilton
London

Pankhurst

Titles in the Profiles *series*

Muhammad Ali	0-241-10600-1	Helen Keller	0-241-11295-8
Chris Bonington	0-241-11044-0	Martin Luther King	0-241-10931-0
Ian Botham	0-241-11031-9	Bob Marley	0-241-11476-4
Geoffrey Boycott	0-241-10712-1	Paul McCartney	0-241-10930-2
Edith Cavell	0-241-11479-9	Lord Mountbatten	0-241-10593-5
Charlie Chaplin	0-241-10479-3	Florence Nightingale	0-241-11477-2
Winston Churchill	0-241-10482-3	Rudolf Nureyev	0-241-10849-7
Sebastian Coe	0-241-10848-9	Emmeline Pankhurst	0-241-11478-0
Roald Dahl	0-241-11043-2	Pope John Paul II	0-241-10711-3
Thomas Edison	0-241-10713-X	Anna Pavlova	0-241-10481-5
Queen Elizabeth II	0-241-10850-0	Prince Philip	0-241-11167-6
The Queen Mother	0-241-11030-0	Lucinda Prior-Palmer	0-241-10710-5
Alexander Fleming	0-241-11203-6	Barry Sheene	0-241-10851-9
Anne Frank	0-241-11294-X	Mother Teresa	0-241-10933-7
Gandhi	0-241-11166-8	Margaret Thatcher	0-241-10596-X
Basil Hume	0-241-11204-4	Daley Thompson	0-241-10932-9
Kevin Keegan	0-241-10594-3	Queen Victoria	0-241-10480-7

First published 1985 by
Hamish Hamilton Children's Books
Garden House, 57-59 Long Acre, London WC2E 9JZ
©1985 text by Linda Hoy
©1985 illustrations by Julian Puckett

British Library Cataloguing in Publication Data

Hoy, Linda
Emmeline Pankhurst. — (Profiles)
1. Pankhurst, Emmeline — Juvenile literature
2. Feminists — Great Britain — Biography —
Juvenile literature
I. Title   II. Series
324.6'23'0924   JN979.P28

ISBN 0-241-11478-0

Typeset by Pioneer
Printed in Great Britain at the
University Press, Cambridge

252398

Contents

1   The Axe Falls

In 1913, as an act of publicity for the suffragettes, a woman threw herself under the feet of the king's horse at the Derby. She was trampled on and hurled some distance across the grass. Her skull was fractured and, two days later, she died without regaining consciousness.

By 1914 over one thousand suffragettes had been in prison for their beliefs. Many of these women went on hunger-strike and some of them also refused to drink. The government was so afraid of suffragettes dying in prison that it insisted they should be force-fed. The women were held down by prison warders whilst long tubes were twisted up their nostrils and forced into their stomachs for liquid food to be poured down.

In March 1914, a suffragette walked into the National Gallery with an axe hidden inside the sleeve of her jacket, held in place by a long chain of safety pins. After spending some time pretending to sketch the Velasquez 'Venus', she slid the axe from her sleeve, ran to the painting and, having broken the glass, attacked it four times with her axe. She said afterwards that she had 'tried to destroy the picture of the most beautiful woman in mythological history as a protest against the

A hunger striker being force-fed

government for destroying Mrs Pankhurst, who is the most beautiful character in modern history.'

*   *   *

Who then were the suffragettes? Why were they prepared to go to such lengths to publicise their cause? And who was Mrs Pankhurst?

The word 'suffrage' means the right to vote in elections. Suffragettes were women who demanded the vote. At one time, only the richest landowners were allowed to elect the government. During the early part of the nineteenth century rallies and protest meetings were held by the Chartists, which led to the vote being widened to include other classes of men.

Women, however, had very few rights. A Victorian father was the head of his household and everything he said was law; his wife and children were expected to obey him. Before 1870, a married woman was not legally allowed to keep any money that she earned herself. Before 1882, anything a woman owned became her husband's when she married.

As time went on, laws were passed that did help women: after 1888 women were allowed to vote in local elections and, after 1907, they could become local councillors. In spite of these changes, however, many women felt insulated at being classed with lunatics, idiots, criminals and children. These were the main groups thought to be incapable of deciding who should govern them. To be recognised as citizens in their own right, women had to be given the vote.

2 Home Life

Emily Pankhurst was the leader of the suffragettes. She was born Emmeline Goulden in 1858, the eldest and favourite daughter of Robert Goulden, an astute businessman who began work as an errand boy and later succeeded in buying his own calico-printing works. He owned a large house with extensive grounds on the outskirts of Manchester and a theatre in Salford, yet he was also eager to improve the lives of the poor. He became involved with the Liberal Party and he and his wife both worked hard in the campaign for the abolition of slavery. One of Emily's earliest memories was of trotting round one of their public meetings with a little bag to collect money for the anti-slavery campaign.

Emily was born into a family which was already sympathetic to the idea of votes for women. Emily's mother took the *Women's Suffrage Journal* every week and when the editor of the paper, Lydia Becker, came to speak in Manchester, Emily begged to be allowed to go with her mother to listen. Although only fourteen, the speeches excited Emily so much that by the time she left the meeting, she had already decided to devote herself to the campaign for women's suffrage.

Middle-class Victorian families saved up to send their clever sons to college, but cared little about the education of their daughters. Most of their schooling was simply to teach them how to make themselves and their homes attractive to men. Emily resented the fact that her brothers' education was considered more important than hers, and she nagged at her father to send her to a better school. By the age of fifteen she was successful; she was sent to a progressive women's college in Paris where she learned subjects such as book-keeping and science. She also learned to dress elegantly and to speak good French.

A short time after her return to England, Emily met Dr Pankhurst. The Doctor was an exciting fiery man with an untidy appearance, a pointed beard and his pockets always crammed with books and papers. He seemed to enjoy shocking respectable society by claiming that God did not exist, that the House of Lords should be abolished and that women should be allowed to vote. It was Dr Pankhurst, in fact, who had drafted the first women's suffrage bill which was presented to Parliament in 1870.

Emily found Dr Pankhurst romantic and inspiring. Her parents admired him and, even though the Doctor had very little money, he and Emily were married in 1879 when she was twenty years old and he was forty. Life for Emily then became an exciting round of public meetings and rallies. With her new husband she joined all kinds of political campaigns and met many different people.

This new phase of her life, however, did not last long. In 1880 her first daughter, Christabel, was born and in 1882 she gave birth to a second daughter, Sylvia. The following year, Dr Pankhurst stood as an Independent parliamentary candidate in Manchester. He thought the Liberal Party would support him but, when they heard him calling for votes for all men and women, for the common ownership of land, the abolition of the House of Lords and Home Rule for the Irish, they refused. Dr Pankhurst was defeated.

To fight an election was expensive and afterwards, when they were short of money, Emily asked her father for help. When Mr Goulden said no, Emily refused to speak to him again. Sadly, she never learned how to make up quarrels. Emily even refused to speak to her mother again until many years later — after her father had died.

The unpleasantness probably made Emily want to leave. She also felt that, in Manchester, her husband's talents were not really appreciated. Even though she now had another child to look after — her first son, Frank — she persuaded her husband in 1885 to move to London.

Shortly afterwards the Doctor was invited by the Liberal Party to stand for Parliament — this time as a candidate for Rotherhithe in London. Also campaigning was Helen Taylor, a new-style feminist who wore something never heard of before for Victorian ladies — a pair of trousers. Emily was shocked and warned her

Emily as a younger woman

husband not to be seen in public with Miss Taylor. The
voters were already horrified to hear that the Doctor
didn't believe in God — to see him walking with a
woman in trousers would be just too much.

The Doctor was a more popular candidate in London
than he had been in Manchester but, in spite of Emily's
help and support, he failed to win the election.

3   To the Workhouse

Emily wanted to earn some money for herself and she bought a fancy goods shop called *Emerson's* in Hampstead. In the 1880s, unlike today, Hampstead was one of the poorer parts of London and Emily, with her ladylike ways, was out of touch with the people who lived there. She tried to sell them things that were fashionable but not much use and too expensive, such as little milking stools enamelled in pastel colours with hand-painted floral designs. There was little demand for ornamental milking stools in Hampstead.

Before very long, the Pankhurst nursery began to fill up with left-overs from *Emerson's*. There was a cardboard model of Tower Bridge with holes for busy little fingers to sew through in cross-stitch. Emily's daughter, Sylvia, woke early one Christmas morning to find beside her bed an oblong box covered with red plush. She could hardly wait to open it. She felt sure the box would contain the present she'd been wanting so badly — a violin. When the time came, Sylvia could hardly hold back her tears — the box was empty. It was a case to keep her gloves in, yet another unsold item from *Emerson's*.

Emily had little time for her children when they

were young. She looked after her eldest child, Christabel, herself and made it obvious that she was her favourite. The other children were handed over to a nurse. Sylvia was punished for failing to eat her cold, lumpy porridge and tied to her bed all day for refusing her cod liver oil, but Christabel was seldom punished. Poor Sylvia's second-hand bike was made from pieces of gas piping welded together; she had a hard time keeping up with Christabel on her brand-new bike with fancy gears when they went out cycling together.

In other ways, the Pankhurst children had an exciting childhood. They met famous interesting people who were frequent visitors to the house and their parents talked to them seriously about politics and religion, treating them like sensible adults.

In 1889 the Pankhursts and their friends formed the Women's Franchise League. Emily's role was as a hostess, giving help and support to her husband. She found it an ordeal to have to introduce the speaker at a talk or to give out a list of announcements. The aim of the League was to obtain the vote for women but it took on too many other issues such as trade unionism and Dr Pankhurst's plan to abolish the House of Lords. Their members found this too confusing and by 1893 the League was abandoned.

Before very long, *Emerson's* was losing so much money that it had to be sold. It was the beginning of a sad time for the Pankhursts because other tragedies were in store: in 1888 four-year-old Frank died from diphtheria and, shortly afterwards, Emily became very ill after giving birth to her second son, Harry.

Towards the end of 1892, the lease on their house at Russell Square came to an end. The Pankhursts, who had been too busy with their many campaigns to bother about house repairs, suddenly found that there were more repairs than they could afford. Worries about money, together with the strain of overwork, made Dr Pankhurst ill. Emily was also run down. The family moved for a brief rest to the seaside town of Southport before going back to live in Manchester.

*   *   *

During the winter of 1894, there were many people out of work. In those days there was no social security for the unemployed, many of whom began to starve. In Manchester Dr Pankhurst organised help for them. Mrs Pankhurst visited the local grocers and market-stall holders each morning asking for gifts of food. Members of the newly-formed Labour Party used the food to make huge pans of soup which they then transported to the town square in removal lorries. Emily and her family helped to serve food to two thousand people a day.

The Pankhursts joined the Labour Party who then voted Emily on to the local board of poor law guardians. These were people who supervised the nearby work-house — an institution for poor people who had no families to support them.

When Emily saw the workhouse she was shocked. The men in charge she described as guardians, not of the poor, but of the rates — always trying to save

Emily with her husband, Dr Pankhurst

money but then wasting it because of inefficiency. The poor people were fed on dry bread; little girls wearing thin, short-sleeved dresses had to scrub the floors, and old people had to sit on plain benches with no backs.

Emily wasted little time in changing this. She said that bread should be cut into slices and spread with margarine and the left-overs made into milk puddings for the elderly. The children should be dressed in warmer clothing and the little girls supplied with nightdresses. Old people were given Windsor chairs

with backs. Emily said: 'In five years' time we had
chang__ ___ __ A modern
schoo__ ___hed at the
workh___ ___ought for
holida__

Emi__ ___do things,
not jus__ ___an in her
own ri__ ___firm and
efficien__ ___rm when
it suit__ ___s of the
workho__

[handwritten note:] After husband died she
and other women decided
to form a new organisation
for women's suffrage to
be called "The women's social
and political union" in
october 1903.

In 1898 _____ __ another tragedy. She had
travelled to France with Christabel to stay with an old
schoolfriend. Shortly afterwards she received a telegram
asking her to come straight home. On the train back to
Manchester, people were reading black-bordered copies
of the local evening paper; on the front page was the
news that Dr Pankhurst was dead.

Back home, Emily learned that the Doctor had been
suffering for some time with stomach ulcers; his doctor
hadn't wanted to tell him that one day one of these
might perforate his stomach and kill him.

The following Saturday there was a great procession
to the cemetery of representatives from all the many
movements in which Dr Pankhurst had worked. The
streets were lined with people as it passed by. Emily
had lost a much-loved husband and Manchester had
lost a highly-respected citizen.

4   The Trail Begins

Dr Pankhurst left no money when he died. Books and furniture were sold to pay off his debts and the family moved to a smaller house. Emily had to earn a living. She became a part-time registrar of births and deaths and that meant, reluctantly, giving up her voluntary work as a poor law guardian.

Emily's work with the poor had taught her a great deal. In particular, she realised that many of the women in the workhouse were there because laws made only by men were biased against women. A man whose wife had died, for instance, would usually have a pension; but if a man died, there would be no pension for his widow. If there could be women in Parliament they would make sure that women's needs were taken care of, but before women could become MPs, they must be given the vote.

*   *   *

In October 1903 Emily invited a number of women to her house in Nelson Street. They decided to form a new organisation for women's suffrage to be called 'The Women's Social and Political Union'. Only women

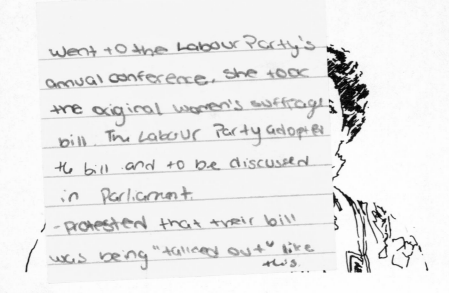

Went to the Labour Party's
annual conference. She took
the original women's suffrage
bill. The Labour Party adopted
th bill .and to be discussed
in Parliament.
- protested that their bill
was being "talked out" like
this.

Christabel and Emily

would be allowed to join.

Meetings were held weekly in the Pankhursts' drawing-room. Thirty or forty women came during the first twelve months and most of the organisation was done by Mrs Pankhurst and her eldest daughter, Christabel, now aged twenty-four.

The following spring, Emily went to the Labour Party's annual conference. She took with her a copy of the original women's suffrage bill which had been drafted by her husband. To her delight, the Labour Party adopted the bill as part of its programme and one MP asked for it to be discussed in Parliament the following May.

Throughout the country, women raised their hopes. Meetings were held and petitions sent around. On Friday, May 12th, a huge gathering of women crowded into the Lobby of the House of Commons to support the passage of their bill. There was much excitement.

The matter to be discussed beforehand was roadway lighting. A bill had been put forward suggesting that carts travelling on the roads at night should be fitted with lights at the back as well as at the front. MPs made the debate on this last as long as possible. They kept telling jokes and silly stories just to make sure there would be no time left to discuss the women's suffrage bill.

When they realised that their bill was being 'talked out' like this, the women in the Lobby became angry. Mrs Pankhurst led them outside to form a protest meeting. They were moved on twice by the police before finally being allowed to stand and listen to speeches condemning the Tory government for not even bothering to discuss the important issues of women's votes.

*　　　　*　　　　*

In 1905 there was to be a general election. The Liberal Party were organising meetings and rallies throughout the country but, nowhere in their programme or their speeches, did they make any mention of votes for women. Emily and Christabel Pankhurst decided that the Liberals should be asked why not.

On October 13th 1905, Sir Edward Grey was to be the main speaker at a big Liberal rally at the Free Trade Hall in Manchester. Christabel and a new recruit to the Women's Social and Political Union — a mill worker called Annie Kenny — made a white banner on which they painted the slogan: *Votes for Women.* They knew what was likely to happen. 'We shall sleep in prison tonight,' Christabel said to her mother before she left.

The hall was crowded as Annie and Christabel listened to the speeches. Then members of the public were invited to ask questions. Several men did so and their questions were answered politely. Then Annie raised her hand. 'Will the Liberal government give votes to women?' she asked.

Annie was ignored. The little white banner was unfurled as Christabel repeated the question. All they received were jeers and catcalls from the crowd. Then a steward walked across and asked Annie to put her question in writing. This she did, but when the paper was passed to Sir Edward he only smiled and passed it on.

The meeting was drawing to a close. The speaker was thanked and people started to get up. Annie, in desperation, stood on her chair and cried out, 'Will the Liberal government give votes to women?'

The crowd became even angrier, shouting at the women, pushing them and jostling. Then the police arrived and quickly led Annie and Christabel outside. Not wanting to give up, they held a protest meeting outside the hall. This time they were both arrested.

In court the women refused to pay their fines. There was no option for the court but to send them to prison: Christabel for one week and Annie for three days.

5 The Lead is Taken

The *Daily Mail* the following morning said: 'If any argument were required against giving to ladies political status, it has been furnished in Manchester.' Most other newspapers carried articles criticising Annie and Christabel's protest but the following week these were followed by readers' letters of support.

When Christabel left Strangeways prison on Friday, October 20th, the scene was described in the *Manchester Evening Chronicle*:

> Miss Pankhurst fell into the arms of her mother, and the two wept with joy after having been parted for a whole week. Mrs Pankhurst asked the people not to forget the principle for which her daughter had suffered. They must press forward and never rest, especially the women, until the vote had been secured. The party then boarded a cab and drove away amidst the cheers of the crowd.

That evening they all attended a meeting held in Annie and Christabel's honour at the Free Trade Hall — from which they had been ejected only a week before. The meeting was filled to overflowing. Kier Hardy, the Labour Party leader, gave an emotional speech of

W.S.P.U. leaders and their motor-car. Seated, Mrs Pankhurst and Miss Annie Kenney. Standing, Mrs Pethick-Lawrence

welcome and Annie and Christabel were presented with bouquets of flowers.

It was the first time that most people had ever heard of the Women's Social and Political Union, which received a sudden rush of new members. The women's suffrage movement had gained more publicity from this one event than it had in all the previous years put together.

*   *   *

The WSPU next launched a campaign of heckling. Members called out and interrupted important politicians when they were making speeches. One of their main targets was the parliamentary candidate, Winston Churchill. Emily Pankhurst described what would happen at his meetings:

"'One great question,' Mr Churchill would exclaim, "remains to be settled."

"And that is women's suffrage," shouts a voice from the gallery.

Mr Churchill struggles on with his speech: "The men have been complaining of me . . ."

"The women have been complaining of you too, Mr Churchill," comes back promptly from the back of the hall.

"In the circumstances what can we do but . . ."

"Give votes to women.'"

There had been all kinds of women's suffrage societies since the 1860s but their members had always been ladylike — politely writing letters, visiting their MPs and organising garden parties or musical evenings. Never before had women used the same political tactics as men: making speeches, heckling politicians and giving out leaflets in the street.

*　　　*　　　*

Emily's second daughter, Sylvia, was a student in London. Annie Kenney was sent to stay with her to spread the campaign to the capital. When Emily went to visit them two weeks later, she found they had booked

Mrs Pankhurst with Mrs Pethick-Lawrence, giving orders to start
the first women's suffrage procession to London, 1906

the Caxton Hall, Westminster, for a huge rally. Emily
gladly helped with the publicity. She gave out leaflets
in the street, chalked notices on pavements and walked
around knocking on doors, inviting women along.

On February 19th, 1906, the date for the opening of
the new parliament, there was the first women's suffrage
procession in London. Three or four hundred women
took part and Emily was moved to tears as she saw them
all standing in line waiting for the orders to start.

The procession made its way to Westminster. Caxton
Hall was filled and the meeting highly successful. At

the same time, the King's speech was being read in Parliament. This outlined the plans of the Liberal Party for their next session. News came to Emily, sitting in Caxton Hall, that the King's speech had made no mention of votes for women. She stood and announced this to the meeting. Then she suggested that the whole body of women should leave Caxton Hall, walk across to the House of Commons and complain.

The women lost no time in following. When they arrived at the House of Commons they found that, for the first time ever, its doors had been barred to women. It was pouring down with rain and bitterly cold, but the women were determined not to leave. Eventually, the government agreed to allow groups of women — twenty at a time — to enter and speak to their MPs. Not one member of Parliament would agree to take up their case.

The women were disappointed but, to Emily, the event had been a great success: the women had risen and followed her to the House of Commons; they had defied the police in refusing to go home. Emily saw her potential as a leader; she had the power to move other women to actions they would not have done before. When women were prepared to stand up and fight for their rights, Emily believed there was nothing they could not achieve.

6 First Time in Prison

In June 1906, Christabel moved to London to become the political organiser of the WSPU. She stayed with the Union's new treasurer, Mrs Pethick-Lawrence and her husband at their house at Clement's Inn — a visit which was to last five years. Emily Pethick-Lawrence treated Christabel like her own daughter and their large house, near the centre of London, became the Union's new headquarters. More and more women volunteered to help in the offices — to type, address envelopes and add up the donations that came pouring in.

It was still Emily Pankhurst, however, who gave the WSPU its leadership and inspiration. At public meetings she spoke with such conviction and persuasion that afterwards women would rush forward with their shilling (5p) subscription, eager to join the WSPU.

One criticism Emily met, however, was that she allowed no one to disagree with her. If members didn't like her ideas then they would be asked to leave. Emily herself chose which women were to be leaders; there were no votes and no elections. Not only was Emily the leader of the WSPU, but its constitution and its book of rules as well.

Mrs Pankhurst addressing a by-election crowd

*   *   *

Whilst Christabel organised the WSPU in London, other suffragettes toured the country with Emily. They booked halls and schoolrooms, hired lorries to address the crowds from, or just took along a soap box to the market square. People found the suffragettes popular and entertaining speakers. During by-elections it was not unusual for them to speak to packed-out meetings and the Liberals to almost empty halls. There was one by-election, however, where they were less than popular. Mid-Devon had been a Liberal stronghold but, with Emily speaking against them, the Liberal

Party was defeated.

After the count at the polls, Emily was walking back to her lodgings with her friend, Mrs Martel, when suddenly, around the corner they were confronted by a crowd of young men wearing the Liberal Party's red rosettes, furious because their party had been defeated. 'They did it!' they yelled at Emily and Mrs Martel. 'Those women did it.'

They shouted abuse and pelted the women with clay and rotten eggs. Emily and her friend rushed into a nearby grocer's shop. The grocer's wife bolted the door behind them, but then her husband cried out that his shop would be wrecked if they stayed there. He took them through the back door into a yard, but as Emily and Mrs Martel ran through, they were ambushed. The crowd of thugs had got there first. They began beating Mrs Martel over the head with their fists. Fortunately, the grocer's wife came out and, with Emily's help, managed to drag Mrs Martel back towards the house; but at the back door Emily was struck suddenly from behind. She fell to the ground and blacked out. Slowly, she became aware of cold, wet mud seeping through her clothing. She looked up and saw the angry circle of drunken youths slowly closing in on her.

Fortunately, at the next moment, the police arrived. The mob turned and fled and Emily was carried into the shop. It was some time before she or Mrs Martel recovered completely from their injuries.

*   *   *

Christabel, Mrs Drummond and Mrs Pankhurst in the dock, first
conspiracy trial, October 1908

On her return to London, Emily tried again to speak to
members of Parliament. The police insisted that she
and her companions walk towards the House of
Commons in single file but Emily, whose ankle still
hurt after her injury in Devon, asked her friends to
take her arms and help her to walk. For this she was
arrested on entering Parliament Square.

The following morning the police court at Westminster
was told that the women had set off with noisy songs
and shouts, assaulting policemen and knocking off their

helmets as they walked along. When Emily protested that none of this was true, she was interrupted and told that she must promise to keep the peace or go to prison for six weeks. Emily went to Holloway.

Prisons at the turn of the century were filthy, cold, dark and stuffy and the food was terrible. For a lady like Emily, always smartly dressed with her hair tied neatly under one of her fashionable hats, to be made to wear prison clothes was a dreadful indignity. To wash in the prison's filthy water made her feel sick. In her own words she describes her arrival at Holloway:

Obeying an order to undress, I took off my gown and then paused. 'Take off everything,' was the next order. 'Everything?' I faltered. It seemed impossible that they expected me to strip. In fact, they did allow me to take off my last garments in the shelter of a bathroom. I shivered myself into some frightful underclothing, old and patched and stained, some coarse, brown woollen stockings with red stripes, and the hideous prison dress stamped all over with the broad arrow of disgrace. I fished a pair of shoes out of a big basket of shoes, old and mostly mismates. A pair of coarse but clean sheets, a towel, a mug of cold cocoa, and a thick slice of brown bread were given to me and I was conducted to my cell.

Emily was troubled by the cold — she had brought a fur coat but was not allowed to wear it. After a few days she became ill and was sent to the prison hospital. The first night she was kept awake by moaning and crying from the next room. In a cold and dreary cell without

Mrs Pankhurst and Christabel in prison dress

any comfort or support, a woman was giving birth to a baby. Emily was horrified. When women won the vote, she determined such conditions would no longer be allowed.

*   *   *

The day before Emily was expected to return, the

WSPU were holding a big meeting at the Albert Hall. On the empty chairperson's seat was a label: *Mrs Pankhurst's Chair*. No one knew that Emily had been released a day early. She entered the meeting after everyone else, walked across to her chair, removed the placard and sat down. A great cry went up around the hall as women stood and stretched their hands towards her. Emily was so moved at her welcome that she could hardly bring herself to speak.

7 Stones Through the Window

Shortly after Emily's release from prison, the Home Secretary — Herbert Gladstone — gave a speech on women's suffrage. Commenting on other campaigns, like the Chartists, he said, 'The people . . . were not content with enthusiastic meetings in large halls; they assembled in their tens of thousands all over the country. Of course,' he added, 'it is not to be expected that women can assemble in such masses, but power belongs to the masses, and through this power a government can be influenced into more effective action.'

The WSPU were stirred to action. They prepared for the largest demonstration ever in Hyde Park. They spent a thousand pounds, a great deal of money in those days, on publicity. They pasted posters in all the major towns; they chalked announcements on pavements, gave out leaflets in the street and walked up and down with sandwich boards. Some of them hired and decorated a motor launch and sailed up the Thames to the Houses of Parliament where members were taking their tea on the terrace. MPs and their guests left their tables and crowded to the water's edge. Then a voice from the boat called out: 'Come to the park on Sunday.

Interviewed by a reporter on the way to the
House of Commons

You shall have police protection and there will be no
arrests, we promise you.' Someone telephoned for the
police launch but, before it could arrive, the women
had steamed away.

On June 21st, 1908, Emily Pankhurst led the first of
seven separate processions to Hyde Park. As she
mounted the steps to the platform and looked around,
she could hardly believe the number of people that
were there — certainly more than the two hundred and
fifty thousand they had hoped for. Speakers in those
days did not have microphones so they had built twenty
different platforms with speakers at each one so that

people could hear more easily. At five o'clock bugles sounded, resolutions were passed calling on the government to bring in a women's suffrage bill without delay and the great chant, 'Votes for Women, Votes for Women' was taken up by the crowd. The *Daily Express* reported next day that: 'It is probable that so many people never before stood in one square mass anywhere in England.'

The government received the women's resolution but still refused to promise them the vote.

Another huge demonstration was held outside Parliament on June 30th. A hundred thousand women desperately tried to make their way, in small groups, through barriers of policemen into the House of Commons. The struggle lasted until well after midnight and resulted in twenty-nine women being arrested. Two of these had each thrown a stone through the window of the Prime Minister's house in Downing Street.

This stone-throwing marked a new departure for the suffragettes. Until then, their demonstrations had been noisy and boisterous but they had never caused deliberate injury to people or damage to property. The women who threw the stones wrote to Emily from prison, apologising for having acted without her orders. They expected her to be angry but, instead, she went to congratulate them in prison. On their release the WSPU presented them with gold brooches set with flint stones.

*　　　　*　　　　*

An Inspector conducts Mrs Pankhurst to the House of Commons, 1908

The suffragettes decided that on October 13th they would make yet another attempt to enter the House of Commons. Leaflets were produced by the Pankhursts saying: 'Men and Women, Help the Suffragettes to Rush the House of Commons, on Tuesday Evening, October 13th, at 7.30.' On October 12th, Emily, Christabel, and their colleague Mrs Drummond, each received an important legal document:

Information has been laid this day by the Commissioner of Police that you, in the month of October, in the year 1908, were guilty of conduct likely to provoke a breach of the peace by initiating and causing to be initiated, by publishing and causing to be published, a certain handbill, calling upon and inciting the public to do a certain wrongful and illegal act, viz. to rush the House of Commons at 7.30 p.m. on October 13th inst.

The following day they were arrested and taken to court; they were each sentenced to three months imprisonment in Holloway.

*　　　　*　　　　*

Once back in Holloway, Emily told the prison Governor that the suffragettes refused to be treated any longer as common criminals. Instead, they demanded the privileges given to prisoners in the 'first division' — those who had committed no crime except to further their religious or political beliefs. The Governor said that there was nothing he could do; if suffragettes had not been sentenced to the first division by the courts then he was not allowed to move them.

After her release, Emily told her followers that in

Mrs Pankhurst recovering from hunger-strike

future they should all refuse to accept the prison rules until suffragettes were treated as political prisoners.

In 1909, one of the suffragettes, on entering Holloway, announced that she would eat no food unless she was transferred into the first division. After she had starved herself for ninety-one hours, the prison authorities set her free. Before very long, more and more women followed her example. These hunger-strikes brought the suffragettes much sympathy. The

Home Secretary, however, was worried. If any women died in prison, he would be blamed; on the other hand, he could not just set them free whenever they went without food. Under pressure from the King, he made a terrible decision: hunger-striking suffragettes would, in future, be fed by force.

Force-feeding involved up to half a dozen wardresses holding down a prisoner whilst a doctor forced a long tube up her nostrils or down her throat into her stomach. Liquid food was then funnelled into the tube. The treatment caused constant vomiting and terrible pain to women who were already weak from starvation.

8   War is Declared

Early in 1910, a group of MPs from the main political parties put together what became known as the Conciliation Bill. This would give the vote to all women who were householders. To show their support, Emily called a truce — the WSPU would do nothing to upset the government whilst the bill went through Parliament. They also organised a march to support the bill. In front were 617 women, dressed in white, carrying long silver poles tipped with broad arrows. These were the suffragettes who had so far suffered imprisonment; they were warmly cheered as they marched along the route to the Albert Hall.

The bill passed its second reading in the House of Commons with a majority of 109. The women were much encouraged and felt sure that, at last, some of them would get the vote.

The main speakers against the bill were Lloyd George and Winston Churchill. They said that to give the vote only to householders was unfair on women who rented property, or who lived with relatives, or in lodgings. The Prime Minister, Mr Asquith, also spoke against the bill: 'No suffrage measure will be satis-factory,' he said, 'which does not give women votes on

Over 1,000 women had suffered imprisonment — Broad Arrows
in the 1910 parade

precisely the same terms as men.' The WSPU were furious. For them it was much better for some women to have the vote than none at all; and, in spite of what the Prime Minister had said, they could see little chance of a Liberal government giving them the vote on equal terms with men.

At a crowded meeting in the Albert Hall, Emily explained that the Prime Minister had said that women's suffrage would not be debated again until the next Parliament — in several years' time. Christabel announced: 'It is an insult to common sense. We hurl it back upon them. They have been talking of declarations of war. We also declare war from this moment.'

And war it was. With a tremendous outburst of cheering, women surged out of the Albert Hall. Some of them rushed to the Houses of Parliament; others followed Emily to Downing Street. The police were not expecting a big demonstration and were standing only two deep across the entrance. Mrs Pankhurst walked straight into the middle of them. The combined force of the hundreds of women behind her soon had the police cordon in pieces. A great cheer went up as the women broke through the gap and charged right up to the house of the Prime Minister. Their success, however, was short-lived. Police reinforcements arrived and, for the next hour, Downing Street and Parliament Square became battlegrounds.

In a letter to the *Daily Mirror* a few days later, the Vice-President of the Royal College of Surgeons described the scene he had witnessed:

> The women were treated with the greatest brutality. They were pushed about in all directions and thrown down by the police. Their arms were twisted until they were almost broken. Their thumbs were forcibly bent back, and they were tortured in other nameless ways that made one feel sick at the sight.

November 18th became known as Black Friday. For many women, the violence shown towards them on that day marked the end of their peaceful struggle. Their actions afterwards became increasingly militant, showing their frustration with a government which persistently refused to listen to their demands.

The head of the deputation on Black Friday, November 1910

*   *   *

On March 2nd, 1912, hundreds of women swarmed through the West End of London armed with stones and hammers. They smashed windows in Regent Street, Piccadilly, the Strand and Oxford Street, causing thousands of pounds worth of damage. Three women, including Emily Pankhurst, leaped out of a car in Downing Street and threw stones at the Prime Minister's house. They broke four panes of glass. The women were arrested and led away but, as they passed the Home Office, Mrs Pankhurst suddenly broke free and threw another stone at one of the windows there. About a hundred and twenty women were arrested altogether.

Three days later, police and detectives descended on Clements Inn with a warrant for the arrest of Christabel and Emily Pankhurst and Mrs and Mrs Pethick-

Lawrence who were charged with: 'Conspiring to incite certain persons to commit malicious damage to property.' During the confusion, Christabel escaped. She fled to Paris and led the WSPU from there until the others came out of prison.

Emily and the Pethick-Lawrences received sentences of nine months each. They were treated as political prisoners with comfortable furniture, their own clothes and writing materials, but when they asked if other suffragettes were also being transferred to the first division, the answer was no. In protest, they began to hunger-strike. News was passed to other prisons and within a short time, eighty other suffragettes had joined the hunger-strike.

As Emily Pankhurst lay in her cell, weak from starvation, she heard sudden screams from Mrs Pethick-Lawrence's cell. She knew that her friend was being forcibly fed. Later, the doctor and wardresses barged into her own cell. 'Instantly' she said, 'I caught up a heavy earthenware jug from a table hard by, and with hands that now felt no weakness I swung the jar head high. "If any of you dares so much as to take one step inside this cell I shall defend myself," I cried. Nobody moved or spoke for a few seconds, and then the doctor confusedly muttered something about tomorrow doing as well, and they all retreated.'

Such a massive hunger-strike caused much concern and questions were asked in Parliament about the dangers of force-feeding. There were cases where food had been poured into women's lungs, almost choking them to death and causing pneumonia and pleurisy.

The argument of the broken window pane

Mr Lansbury, a friend of the suffragettes, was sent out of the House of Commons for confronting the Prime Minister. 'Sir,' he said, 'you are beneath contempt. You call yourselves gentlemen, and you forcibly feed and murder women in this fashion. You ought to be driven out of office. It is the most disgraceful thing that ever happened in the history of England. You will go down in history as the men who tortured innocent women.'

No other attempts were made to forcibly feed either Mrs Pankhurst or Mrs Pethick-Lawrence and within two days they were released from prison on grounds of ill health. Before very long, the other suffragettes were released as well.

9 Women in the Post

By 1912 the Women's Social and Political Union had grown into a huge organisation. Most of the work was done by volunteers but there were still 110 officials on the payroll — many of whom were based in the twenty-one rooms now occupied at Clements Inn. By the end of 1911 there were thirty-six branches of the Union in London alone — ten of these having their own shops. The income of the WSPU had risen from £3,000 in 1906-7 to £29,000 in 1910-11 and it had a weekly newspaper, *Votes for Women,* with a circulation of nearly 40,000.

The Union produced clever publicity material. As well as postcards, posters and badges, for example, they made a suffragette card game called *Panko* and a dice game similar to Snakes and Ladders called *Suffragettes In and Out of Prison.*

One of the Union's greatest strengths was the use it made of publicity. It aimed to keep the slogan, *Votes for Women* always in the public eye by making news which journalists would want to write about. Some of the stories, like the hunger-strikes, meant terrible suffering; others were more light-hearted.

In 1909 it became possible to post human letters and

The re-arrest of Mrs Pankhurst, May 1913

the WSPU decided to post some suffragettes to the Prime Minister. Three women were despatched from the post office in the Strand; they were escorted by a messenger to 10 Downing Street and arrived carrying a *Votes for Women* placard. The Prime Minister said that he did not want to receive his 'correspondence' and asked for the mail to be 'returned to sender'. The women claimed that, as they had been paid for in advance, he would have to accept them. An argument followed which resulted in the suffragettes returning to Clements Inn, but they had provided the newspapers with an entertaining story and the photographs which appeared in the papers next day showed the *Votes for Women* placard prominently displayed.

*   *   *

With such a large organisation and so much publicity it is difficult to understand why, by 1912, the WSPU had not been successful. Many people in those days — men in particular — were horrified at the thought of women gaining the vote. As one man put it: 'Votes for women, indeed: we shall be asked next to give votes to our horses and dogs.'

Attitudes were slow to change. Women had been brought up to think of themselves as inferior to men and sadly, when people are discriminated against like this, they achieve very little. Experiments have shown, for example, that when teachers are told that their pupils are stupid, they expect such poor work from them that the pupils often fail. Because people expected women to be stupid, frail and dependent on men, that was how they behaved. Many women themselves believed that they weren't clever enough to understand politics. Some of them even joined anti-suffrage societies — to campaign against getting the vote.

The suffragettes, of course, were impatient. Women

A suffragette's demonstration. A bag of flour is thrown at Mr Asquith

had been working to get the vote for the last forty-five years — they had campaigned in every peaceful way they could think of, but success did not seem any nearer.

At this stage, the Women's Social and Political Union became divided. Emily and Christabel Pankhurst decided that peaceful methods had got them nowhere and drew up a plan for a much more violent campaign.

They would start attacking and destroying property and breaking more windows. The government, they said, would then be forced to give in to their demands.

The Pethick-Lawrences thought this new plan not only wrong but foolish. If the suffragettes behaved like criminals, people would say they were irresponsible and did not deserve to vote. They argued that the best way forward was to have more big demonstrations and try to educate people — to show them that women were as capable and intelligent as men.

*　　　　*　　　　*

Two weaknesses of Emily Pankhurst's were that she seldom listened to anyone else's point of view and she was hopeless at making up quarrels. She refused to budge from the plan that Christabel had drawn up and, when the Pethick-Lawrences would not accept it, she refused to speak to them again. The Lawrences were devastated. Even Christabel, who had lived at their house for so many years, had been on holiday with them and was treated like their own daughter, now became a complete stranger. 'The Pankhursts,' they said, 'did nothing by halves!'

10　The Cat and Mouse Act

When she launched the new campaign, Emily urged her followers: 'Be militant each in your own way,' and this they did. Golf courses were one of their first targets. The turf was burned with acid, in some cases spelling out *Votes for Women*. Next the suffragettes broke street lamps, set fire to letter-boxes, slashed the cushions of railway carriages, painted *Votes for Women* on the seats at Hampstead Heath and painted out house numbers on the streets.

Many followers did not agree with the new policy. Emily said: 'I get letters from people who tell me that they do not like the recent developments in the militant movement, and implore me to urge the members not to be reckless with human life.'

Emily argued that human life was not endangered by the new plan but there was no way in which the leaders of the WSPU could keep the vandalism in control. Bombs were planted in empty houses and unused railway stations. Massive fires were started. The orchid houses at Kew were wrecked and many precious flowers died of the cold. The Jewel Room at the Tower of London was broken into and one of the showcases broken. The restaurant in Regents Park was burned

'Cat and Mouse' — A W.S.P.U. poster

down and a new country house which was being built
for Lloyd George was partly destroyed by a bomb.

Four days after this, Emily Pankhurst was once again

arrested. No one suspected her of planting the bomb at Lloyd George's house but, as leader of the organisation, she was held responsible and sentenced to three years imprisonment. Emily said that she would go on hunger-strike. There had been so much outcry about forcible feeding that the government had to find another way of dealing with the suffragettes. They passed a new law which said a hunger-striker could be set free until she put on weight and got better, then taken back to prison again. The law became known as the 'Cat and Mouse Act'.

Emily refused to eat for nine days. 'Towards the end,' she says, 'I was mercifully half-conscious of my surroundings and it was almost without emotion that I heard, on the morning of the tenth day, that I was to be released temporarily to recover my health. The Governor came to my cell and read me my licence, which commanded me to return to Holloway in fifteen days. With what strength my hands retained I tore the document in strips and dropped it on the floor of the cell.'

Whilst Emily was at home recovering, the death occurred of Emily Davison who had thrown herself under the King's horse at the Derby. A huge funeral procession was organised in her honour. Emily Pankhurst was leaving her flat to attend when she was re-arrested by detectives and taken back to Holloway.

This time Emily refused to eat or to drink. The thirst-strike she described as 'simple and unmitigated torture. The body,' she explained, 'cannot endure loss of moisture . . . the skin becomes shrunken and flabby,

Mrs Pankhurst arrested outside Buckingham Palace

the facial appearance alters horribly . . . there is constant headache and nausea, and sometimes there is fever. The mouth and tongue become coated and swollen, and the voice shrinks to a thready whisper.'

During the year 1913, Emily Pankhurst was imprisoned under the Cat and Mouse Act six times. She was fifty-five years old.

*   *   *

In January 1914, another split occurred within the WSPU. Sylvia Pankhurst had been organising the Union in London's East End. She had been deeply moved by the poverty there — by the squalid houses and the terrible work women had to do to earn a few shillings a week. Sylvia worked with the local Labour Party to help people improve their own lives as well as campaigning for the vote.

Emily and Christabel Pankhurst, both now hiding in Paris, sent for Sylvia. They told her that the East London Federation of the WSPU must become a separate organisation. Christabel explained that the WSPU should have no connection with any political party. She also argued that it was a waste of time to recruit women from the poorer working class. 'We want picked women,' she told Sylvia, 'the very strongest and most intelligent.' She also complained that women in the East End Federation were encouraged to organise themselves and allowed to vote at meetings. 'We do not want that,' she said. 'We want all out women to take their instructions and walk in step like an army.'

Sylvia had recently come out of prison after five weeks' hunger-strike and forcible feeding; she had lost eleven kilograms in weight, was extremely weak and

Christabel and Mrs Pankhurst in the garden of Christabel's Paris home

felt too ill to argue. Sadly, she realized that she had lost
for ever the support and friendship of her older sister
and her mother.

11 A Great War Effort

People started to become extremely angry with the suffragettes who were now damaging more buildings, cutting telegraph wires, attacking paintings and setting fire to the politicians' favourite London clubs.

Suffragettes had always been the subject of jokes — men liked to pretend that it was only the unattractive women (those who couldn't find a husband) who joined the WSPU. That was far from true but it caused amusement when, at one meeting for instance, a young man raised a placard saying instead of *Votes for Women*, *Blokes for Women*.

This good-humoured resistance to the suffragettes now disappeared. Women speaking in public were attacked and some had their clothes torn from them. It became less dangerous, but more exciting, to set fire to a building or a post-box than to stand on the street corner and make a speech.

Although the suffragettes were often criticised for damaging property, it is important to remember that they only did this when all other methods seemed to have failed. The women's suffrage campaign started in the 1860s and only between 1912 and 1914 did they use real violence — and only then to property.

It is difficult to guess what would have happened of their militancy had continued: would the government have given in? Or would they have held out even longer? We cannot tell.

In 1914 war was declared with Germany and Emily Pankhurst felt that nothing should interfere with her country's efforts to win. She declared another truce and, in response, the government set free all suffragette prisoners.

*   *   *

Emily was now fifty-six years old and had been through ten hunger-strikes in the last eighteen months. The truce probably saved her life. She and Christabel were able to return from hiding in France without any fear of arrest.

Emily put aside the campaign for women's votes and toured the country urging women to take over men's jobs so they could go and fight in the war. On June 28th, 1915, Lloyd George received a letter from Buckingham Palace saying: 'His Majesty the King was wondering whether it would be possible or advisable for you to make use of Mrs Pankhurst.'

A few days later the WSPU received £2,000 from Lloyd George to help pay for a parade around the slogan, *Women's Right to Serve.* Lloyd George and Winston Churchill inspected the parade of over 30,000 women. The aim of the demonstration was to persuade employers to let women take over men's jobs in industry. It was highly successful.

The campaign made trade unionists very angry. They had been arguing that men and women should be paid the same rates for doing the same job and now women were being employed in the arms factories for much lower wages than men. Sylvia Pankhurst supported the trade unionists and spoke out in public against her mother's campaign. Sylvia felt that women should work with the Socialists for a world without war where men and women of all countries could live together in peace. Her mother was more militant: she believed that it was better to fight the Germans than work for peace and felt that anyone who did not want to help in the war effort was a traitor.

The conflict came to a head on April 8th 1916, when Sylvia, with others who opposed the war, marched from the East End to Trafalgar Square. It was quite a small demonstration but they were set upon by bands of soldiers who tore down their banners and pelted them with screwed up balls of paper filled with paint.

Emily Pankhurst was touring America rallying support for the war when she heard about Sylvia's demonstration. She was very angry. Straightaway she sent a telegram: 'STRONGLY REPUDIATE AND CONDEMN SYLVIA'S FOOLISH AND UNPATRI-OTIC CONDUCT. REGRET I CANNOT PREVENT USE OF NAME. MAKE THIS PUBLIC.'

*   *   *

Recruiting poster

The *Women's Right to Work* campaign was a great success. Women worked in the factories and on the land, they drove ambulances, motor bikes and lorries. Their willingness to take over men's jobs enabled the government, in 1916, to draft all able-bodied men into the armed services.

In 1916, the question of votes for women was once again raised in Parliament. This time Asquith said that women should receive some recognition for the great effort they had made during the war and should be encouraged to help rebuild the country after the war was over. It may also have occurred to him that, if women did not get the vote now, they would soon resume their militant campaign when the war was finished.

On January 10th, a bill was passed which gave the vote to all women over the age of thirty — six times the number that had been suggested before. In 1928, a final law was passed to give the vote to women at twenty-one, the same age as men. There was no opposition to this. Everyone realised by then that women could vote without the world being turned upside down. This new law marked the end of Emily Pankhurst's work. She died very shortly afterwards.

12   The Importance of the Struggle

In spite of the hopes of the suffragettes, it was many years before the vote made any real difference to women. Few women stood for Parliament; even fewer were elected. It was fifty years before a law was passed to say that men and women should have equal pay or that women should not be discriminated against when applying for a job.

Women are grateful for the vote but, for those who actually fought for it, the struggle itself was probably more important than the result. It was not gaining the vote which liberated the suffragettes but the discovery, throughout the long years of their struggle, of strength and determination which they never knew they possessed.

Emily was strong and fearless, a charismatic leader with the faith and dedication to inspire hundreds of thousands of women. Yet it was a weakness of hers that she had to be in charge. Her officers were hand-picked women whom she could trust to carry out her ideas. She would not trust others to work out plans and strategies, or to elect the women they wanted to be leaders.

We must bear in mind, however, that probably the

Mrs Pankhurst's statue in Victoria Tower Gardens

suffragettes could not have been organised in any other way. Women at the turn of the century were used to obeying orders, never thinking for themselves or acting independently. If the WSPU had expected this of them, they might never have joined.

On the other hand, if Emily Pankhurst had encouraged other women to take control of their own lives, they would not only have gained the vote, but discovered within themselves the strength which Emily herself possessed — a strength which would have enabled them to use their new vote to the full.